This Little Tiger book
belongs to:

_____

_____

_____

For Jemma Raeburn
– J W

To my big brother Joe
– M S

LITTLE TIGER PRESS
1 The Coda Centre, 189 Munster Road, London SW6 6AW
www.littletiger.co.uk

First published in Great Britain 2016
This edition published 2016

Text copyright © Jeanne Willis 2016
Illustrations copyright © Matt Saunders 2016
Jeanne Willis and Matt Saunders have asserted their rights to be identified
as the author and illustrator of this work under the Copyright,
Designs and Patents Act, 1988

Printed in China · LTP/1400/1262/0416

2 4 6 8 10 9 7 5 3 1

THERE'S NO SUCH THING AS A SNAPPENPOOP

Jeanne Willis ✳ Matt Saunders

LITTLE TIGER PRESS
London

Big Brother always played the best games.
But the best game of all was . . .
not letting Little Brother join in!

"Can I play?" he said.

"Please let me play!" said Little Brother.

"I'll do anything you say."

"Ok," said Big Brother.

"Go and fetch me a unicorn."

"All right, back soon," said Little Brother.
And off he ran. Through fields and forests.
He was gone for hours.

"That got rid of him!"
laughed Big Brother.
"There are no unicorns."

BUT . . .

. . . Little Brother found one!
Big Brother could not believe his eyes.
"Now can I play?" said Little Brother.

Big Brother shook his head.
"No! It's the wrong kind of unicorn," he said.
"It's too small. You can only play if you fetch
me a lion with wings."

"OK. Whatever you say,"
said Little Brother.
And off he ran. Through
deserts . . .

. . . and jungles. He was gone for days.
"That got rid of him!" laughed Big Brother.

"There's no such thing
as a lion with wings."
But to his AMAZEMENT . . .

. . . Little Brother found one!

"Now can I play?" he said.

Big Brother shook his head.

"No! I wanted a RED lion, not a yellow one, silly."

"Oh," said Little Bro. "You never said."

"Go and fetch me a triceratops instead," said Big Brother.

"Any particular size or colour?" asked Little Brother.

"Big and brown," said Big Brother.

"OK, that narrows it down," said Little Brother.

And off he ran. Through time and space.

He was gone for weeks.

"That got rid of him!"
laughed Big Brother.
"There are no triceratops.
They are extinct!"
BUT . . .

. . . Little Brother
found one!

It was certainly big and certainly brown.
He'd done exactly as he was asked.
"You have to let me play now," he said.
Big Brother thought about it.

"All right," he said. "On one condition."

"What is that?" said Little Brother.

"You must fetch me a Massive Spiny Snappenpoop."

"I've never heard of it," said Little Brother.

"Is it friendly?"

"Imagine the scariest monster times a million!"
said Big Brother. "THAT is a Snappenpoop."

Little Brother wasn't sure he could find one.
But he really wanted to play, so off he ran.
Through shadows and shapes.

"That got rid of him!"
laughed Big Brother. "I'm so clever.
He'll never find the Snappenpoop.
I made it up. There is no such thing!"
BUT . . .

. . . there was!

While Little Brother went looking for the Snappenpoop,
the Snappenpoop came looking for Big Brother.
"My brother will only let me play if I fetch him a
Mini Mouthy Meanie like you," said the Snappenpoop.

"I'm not a Mini Mouthy Meanie!"
said Big Brother.
But whether he was or wasn't, nobody argues
with a Massive Spiny Snappenpoop.

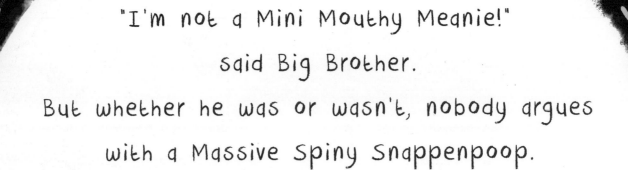

Little Brother returned.

He never found the Snappenpoop. Or Big Brother.

"Now who am I going to play with?" he said.

"Us!" said the unicorn,
the winged lion and the triceratops.

And it was the best game ever!